This book belongs to

Harris
with lots of love
Uncle Stephen, Aunte
Suzy &   Marie-Lorre
                      xx

This volume first published in paperback in Great Britain by HarperCollins Children's Books in 2011

9 10 8

ISBN: 978-0-00-742370-5

HarperCollins Children's Books is a division of HarperCollins Publishers Ltd.

Text copyright © Michael Bond 1984, 1986, 1987, 2003
Illustrations copyright © R. W. Alley 1998, 1999, 2003

Visit our website at: www.harpercollins.co.uk

Printed and bound in China

MICHAEL BOND

Paddington's
London
Treasury

Four classic stories of the bear from Peru

illustrated by R.W. ALLEY

HarperCollins *Children's Books*

Dear Aunt Lucy

As you will see from this book, one of the nicest things about London is that there is never a dull moment.

Love
Paddington

Aunt Lucy
Home for
Retired Bears
Lima
Peru

Contents

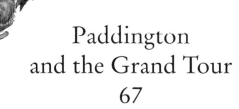

Paddington
at the Palace

One morning Paddington and Mr Gruber set out to see the Changing of the Guard at Buckingham Palace.

Mr Gruber took his camera, Paddington took a flag on a stick in case he saw the Queen, and they both sat on the front seat of the bus so that they could see all the places of interest on the way.

The bus took them most of the way, then they had to walk
through St James's Park.

It was a lovely sunny morning and there were flowers
everywhere.

"I think I may pick some for the Queen," said Paddington.

"I'm afraid that's against the law," said Mr Gruber. "This is what is known as a Royal Park, and all the flowers belong to the Queen anyway. Besides, it would spoil it for others.

"If you like I'll take a picture for your scrapbook instead."

"Fancy having a front garden as big as this," said Paddington. "I wonder if she has to mow the lawn?"

Mr Gruber laughed and then, as they drew near to some large gates, he pointed towards the roof of a building behind them.

"We're in luck's way, Mr Brown," he said. "There's a flag flying. That means the Queen is at home."

Paddington peered through the railings and waved his own flag several times in case the Queen was watching.

"I think I saw someone at one of the windows, Mr Gruber," he called excitedly. "Do you think it was the Queen?"

"Who knows?" said Mr Gruber.

Soon afterwards they heard the sound of a band playing. The music got louder and louder and there was a lot of shouting and the *clump, clump* of marching feet.

But by then there were so many people, Paddington couldn't see a thing.

Mr Gruber wondered whether he ought to suggest holding Paddington up to see, but in the end he bought him a periscope instead.

"If you look through the bottom end," he explained, "you can see over the top of people's heads."

Paddington tried it out, but all he could see were other people's faces and he didn't think much of some of those.

In the end he tried crawling through the legs of the crowd, but by the time he got to the other side the band had passed by.

"Look," said a small boy, pointing at Paddington. "One of the soldiers has dropped his hat."

"It's what they call a busby, dear," said his mother.

Paddington jumped to his feet. "I'm not a *busby*," he cried. "I'm a bear!"

Gradually the crowd melted away until there were only a few people left.

"Oh dear," said Mr Gruber. "It's all over and I didn't even get a picture of you with one of the guardsmen."

"I didn't even *see* them," said Paddington sadly.

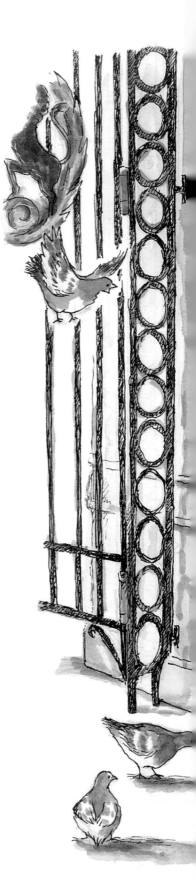

Just then a man in a bowler hat said something to a policeman by the gate, and then pointed towards Paddington and Mr Gruber.

The policeman beckoned to them. "I've instructions to invite you inside so that you can take a proper photograph," he called. "You're very honoured."

Paddington felt most important as he and Mr Gruber followed the policeman across the Palace parade ground and the guard came to attention.

"I think," he said, as he stood to attention while Mr Gruber took a photograph, "this guard is so good he doesn't need changing."

As they left the Palace, Paddington stopped by the gates to wave his flag.

"Do you think it was the Queen looking out of the window when we first came?" he asked.

"It was either the Queen," said Mr Gruber, "or it was someone who likes bears very much."

And he took one last picture for Paddington's scrapbook. "You must mark the window with a cross when you paste it in – just in case."

me at the Palace.

Paddington
at the Zoo

One day Jonathan and Judy decided to take Paddington on an outing to the zoo.

Before they set off Paddington made a large pile of marmalade sandwiches – six in all.

But when they reached the zoo, the gatekeeper wouldn't let them in.

"I'm sorry," he said. "Pets aren't allowed."

"Pets!" repeated Jonathan.

"Paddington isn't a *pet*," said Judy. "He's one of the family."

And Paddington gave the man such a hard stare he let them in without another word.

"Come on," said Jonathan. "Why don't I take your picture with the parrot?"

"Give a great big smile," called Judy. "Say cheese!"

"Cheese," said Paddington.

"Squawk!" said a parrot as it took a big bite out of Paddington's sandwich. "Thank you very much. Squawk! Squawk!"

Next they went to see the Siberian Wild Dog.

"Nice doggie," said Paddington.

But the Siberian Wild Dog went, "Owwowwwowwwoo!" and made Paddington jump so much the rest of the sandwich flew out of his hand and landed in the cage.

"Let me take a picture of you with a donkey," said Jonathan.

"Hee! Haw!" brayed the donkey when it saw Paddington's sandwiches.

"That's two gone," said Judy.

Paddington's smile was getting less cheesy all the time.

The elephant didn't wait to be asked
either. It simply made a loud
trumpeting noise –
"Whoooohoowooo!" –
and reached down
with its trunk.

Paddington watched as his third sandwich disappeared. He
began to feel that going to the zoo was not such a good idea
after all.

But there was worse to follow.

When the lion saw them coming, it gave a great roar –
"Grrrrrrrrahh!"

It was such a loud roar Paddington dropped his fourth sandwich on the ground and before he could say "help" it was surrounded by pigeons.

The only ones who didn't say anything were the penguins. They just stood there looking sad, as if they were all dressed up for a party but had nowhere to go.

Paddington felt so sorry for them he gave them sandwich number five.

"Penguins eat fish," said a man sternly. He pointed to a notice. "It is strictly forbidden to give them marmalade sandwiches."

And while Paddington was looking at the notice, the man helped himself to the last of the sandwiches!

"The cheek of it!" said Jonathan.

"You need eyes in the back of your head," agreed Judy.

"I need my elevenses," said Paddington. "Zoos make you hungry. Besides, nothing more can happen to me now."

But it did. Just to round things off, the mountain goat ate his sandwich bag!

"That does it!" said Jonathan. "If you ask me, it's time we went home."

A few days later Jonathan showed Paddington the photographs he'd taken at the zoo. "You can have one for your scrapbook," he said.

"Which do you like best?" asked Judy.

"The one with the parrot," said Paddington promptly.
"At least he said 'thank you' when he ate my marmalade
sandwich. That's more than any of the others did!"

Paddington
and the
Marmalade Maze

One day, Paddington's friend, Mr Gruber, took him on an outing to a place called Hampton Court Palace.

"I think you will enjoy it, Mr Brown," he said as they drew near. "It's very old and it has over one thousand rooms. Lots of Kings and Queens have lived here."

Paddington always enjoyed his outings with Mr Gruber and he couldn't wait to see inside the Palace.

As they made their way through
an arch, Mr Gruber pointed to
a large clock.

"That's a very special clock," he
said. "It not only shows the time,
it tells you what month it is."

"Perhaps we should hurry, Mr
Gruber," said Paddington anxiously.
"It's half past June already."

They hadn't been inside the Palace very long before they came across a room which had the biggest bed Paddington had ever seen.

"Queen Anne used to sleep in it," said Mr Gruber.

"I expect they put the rope round it to stop her falling out when she had visitors," said Paddington, looking at all the people.

"This is known as the 'Haunted Gallery'," said Mr Gruber.
"They do say that when Catherine Howard's ghost passes by
you can feel a cold draught."

Paddington shivered. "I hope she's got a duffle coat like
mine!" he said.

Mr Gruber took Paddington to see the kitchen next.

"In the old days they used wood fires," he explained. "That's why there is such a high ceiling. There was a lot of smoke."

"I was hoping they might have left some Royal buns behind," said Paddington, licking his lips.

"Talking of buns," said Mr Gruber, "I think it's time we had our lunch."

He led the way outside and they sat down together on the edge of a pool.

As Paddington opened his suitcase he accidentally dropped one of his sandwiches into the water. It was soon alive with goldfish.

"They must like marmalade," said Mr Gruber. "I wonder if that's how they got their name?"

When they had finished their sandwiches, Mr Gruber took
Paddington to see 'The Great Vine'.

"It's very famous," he said. "Every year
they pick over five hundred bunches
of grapes. Imagine that,
Mr Brown!"

"I'm trying to, Mr Gruber," said Paddington. "I think I might plant a grape pip when I get back home."

Mr Gruber chuckled. "I'm afraid you will have a long wait, Mr Brown," he said. "That vine is over two hundred years old."

"Now," said Mr Gruber, "before we leave we must visit the famous maze. Sometimes it takes people hours to find their way out."

"I hope that doesn't happen to us," said Paddington. "My paws are getting tired."

"Perhaps it's time I took you home," said Mr Gruber.

Much to his surprise, the words were no sooner out of his mouth than everyone around them began to talk.

"Hey, that sounds a great idea," said a man in a striped shirt.

"Please to wait while I buy a new film for my camera," said a Japanese lady.

"I've never been inside a real English home before," said another lady. "I wonder if they serve tea?"

"Oh, dear!" whispered Mr Gruber. "They must think I'm one of the guides. What shall we do?"

"Mrs Bird won't be very pleased if they all follow us home," exclaimed Paddington. "She only has a small teapot."

Then he had an idea.

"Follow me," he called. "I think perhaps we ought to go in the maze after all."

"Are you sure we are doing the right thing?" gasped Mr Gruber, as he hurried on behind.

"Bears are good at mazes," said Paddington. "You need to be in Darkest Peru. The forests are very thick."

And sure enough, before Mr Gruber had time to say any more, Paddington led the way out, leaving everyone else inside.

"How ever did you manage to do that, Mr Brown?" gasped
Mr Gruber.

"Quickest visit I've ever seen," agreed the man in the
ticket office.

"I used marmalade chunks to show where we had been,"
said Paddington. "It's something my Aunt Lucy taught me
before she went into the Home for Retired Bears."

"But I thought you had eaten all your sandwiches," said Mr Gruber.

"I always keep a spare one under my hat in case I have an emergency," said Paddington. "That's something else Aunt Lucy taught me. She'll be very pleased when she hears."

And he stopped at a kiosk to buy a picture postcard so that he could write and tell her all about his day out.

That night when he went to bed, as well as the postcard and a pen, Paddington took some rope.

"It's something Queen Anne used to do," he announced. "I've a lot to tell Aunt Lucy and I don't want to fall out of bed before I've finished."

Paddington
and the Grand Tour

One morning Paddington answered the door bell at number thirty-two Windsor Gardens and to his surprise he found his best friend, Mr Gruber, waiting outside.

"I've decided to treat myself to an outing, Mr Brown," he said, "and I was wondering if you would care to join me?"

Paddington was very excited. He always enjoyed his days out with Mr Gruber and he didn't need asking twice.

In no time at all he returned with his suitcase full of marmalade sandwiches ready for the journey, along with Mrs Bird's umbrella in case it rained.

They hadn't gone very far when Paddington spotted a bench.
"Perhaps we ought to eat our sandwiches now, Mr Gruber,"
he said. "If it rains they might get wet."

While they had stopped Mr Gruber showed Paddington
some photographs of the places he wanted to visit.

"I thought we might go on what's called a Hop On – Hop Off bus," said Mr Gruber.

"You can come and go as you like, so it's possible to see lots of different sights with only one ticket."

"I don't think I've ever been on one of those before," said Paddington as they went on their way. "It sounds very good value."

But as they turned a corner and Paddington saw the waiting bus he nearly fell over backwards with alarm, for part of the roof was missing.

"I think the driver must have gone under a low bridge by mistake!" he exclaimed.

Mr Gruber laughed. "Don't worry, Mr Brown. It's made that way so that the passengers have a good view of the sights. If you wait here and form a queue," he continued, "I'll get the tickets. Then we can make sure of seats in the front row."

"That's a good idea," said an inspector. "The early bird catches the worm and I'm expecting a large party of assorted overseas visitors any moment now."

"Perhaps I can interest
you in one of these
booklets telling you all
about the trip," said
the inspector. "It comes
in lots of different
languages."

Paddington was most
impressed. "Thank you
very much," he said.
"I'd like one in
Peruvian, please."

"Peruvian!" repeated
the man. "I'm afraid
we don't get much
call for that."

"You don't get much call for it?" exclaimed Paddington. "Everybody speaks it in Darkest Peru. You don't even have to call out."

He gave the man a hard stare.

"Wait here," said the inspector nervously. "I'll see what I can do."

No sooner had the inspector disappeared than Paddington saw a crowd approaching, so he raised Mrs Bird's umbrella in case he had a job finding him again.

"I'm sorry we're late," panted the leader of the group. "We got held up."

Paddington politely raised his hat. "That's all right," he began. "We can't all be early birds. I'm forming a que…"

Before he had time to say any more he found himself being pushed to one side as there was a mad scramble to board the bus.

Paddington watched in dismay as everyone on the top deck began fighting for the front seats.

"I wouldn't sit there if I were you," he called. "There may still be some worms." But he was wasting his breath, so he tried again. "Excuse me," he called. Lifting one leg, he waved the umbrella. "It's a Hop On bus and I'm afraid the two front seats upstairs are reserved."

"Hold it, you guys!" The leader gave a loud blast on his whistle. "You're supposed to hop everywhere, OK? Pass it down the line."

"What happens now?" came a voice, when everyone was settled.

Paddington considered the matter for a moment. "I'm not sure," he replied. "I shall need to ask Mr Gruber, but I think you look at the view, then you hop off again."

"View?" wailed someone. "What view?"

Their voices were lost in the general commotion as the leader blew several more blasts on his whistle and issued fresh instructions.

"I came on this trip to see the sights," protested a lady as she staggered off the bus, "not become one!"

"I'm worn out," gasped another, collapsing into her husband's arms, "and we haven't been anywhere yet!"
A number of passers-by stopped to watch and several children joined in the fun.

Soon the whole pavement was alive with figures.
Paddington tried closing his eyes, but whenever
he opened them more people had arrived.

He was very relieved when he spied a familiar figure pushing his way through the crowd towards him.

"Are you all right, Mr Brown?" called Mr Gruber. "This place looks like a battlefield."

"It feels like one, Mr Gruber," said Paddington. "I was trying to save our seats in the front row, but I'm afraid I wasn't quick enough."

"The inspector gave me this booklet," said Mr Gruber. "He said he's very sorry it's in English, but he suggested we find somewhere quiet to read it until the fuss had died down. There's a little café over there. I'll hurry on ahead and reserve a table."

Mr Gruber hadn't gone very far before Paddington felt a spot of rain on the end of his nose, so he stopped to open the umbrella. Almost immediately he heard a whistle and a voice shouting, "Follow him, you guys! Don't let him out of your sight!"

Paddington hurried on his way as fast as his legs would carry him. Even so, he only just managed to reach the café ahead of the others.

"Quick, Mr Brown," hissed a voice from behind some potted plants. "Over here. There's some cocoa on its way."

"I should be careful with your sips, Mr Brown," warned Mr
Gruber as the waitress arrived with two steaming mugs.
"It looks very hot and they may give the game away."

"I don't know about my sips, Mr Gruber," gasped Paddington, as the crowd burst through the door. "I'm beginning to wish I'd brought my disguise outfit."

"There you are!" cried the leader. "I've never known a tour captain so hard to keep up with."

"Tour captain?" repeated Paddington.

"You were holding up your umbrella…" said the man. "That's what tour captains always do. It's so that people don't get lost."

"I'm not a tour captain," said Paddington, hotly. "I'm a bear."

The crowd fell silent as they took in the news.

"You mean we've been doing all that hopping around for nothing," complained one of the party. "I thought it was some quaint old English custom."

"What are we going to do now?" cried someone else. "We've missed our bus!"

Paddington looked out of the window at the rain and then at his booklet. "I think I've got an idea coming on," he announced.

After explaining what he had in mind, he waited for the others to settle down. Then, while Mr Gruber held up his pictures one by one, Paddington read from the booklet.

If the words didn't always match up with the pictures no one seemed to mind, and at the end, as the sun came out again, they all applauded.

"That was the best tour I've never been on," said someone amid general agreement.

"I didn't know Buckingham Palace was over sixty metres high," said a lady as the party began to leave.

"I'm afraid it got mixed up with Nelson's Column by mistake," explained Paddington. "It's a bit difficult with paws and I must have turned over two pages at once."

"Never mind," said a man. "The exercise has done us all good. I haven't felt so fit in years."

And to show how pleased they were, everyone dropped a coin or two into Paddington's umbrella as they went past.

"Well," said Mr Gruber, when it was all quiet again. "What do you think of that, Mr Brown?"

"I think," said Paddington, "I might become a tour captain when I'm old enough. It seems a very good job for a rainy day. Especially if you have your own umbrella!"